WOMAN – Your Strength or Your Weakness ???

BookSquirrel Publications

BookSquirrel Publication

Mahadev Totala Nager, Indore (M.P),452001
Regd Under MSME
Website:www.booksquirrelpublication.com

©**Copyright, 2020,** Ishani Agarwal

All rights reserved. No part of this book may be reproduced, stored in a retrieval system, or transmitted, in any form by any means, electronic, mechanical, magnetic, optical, chemical, manual, photocopying, recording or otherwise, without the prior written consent of its writer.

"Woman- Your Strength or Your Weakness"

By: Ishani Agarwal

ISBN: 978-93-89923-91-9

English and Hindi Anthology

Book Formatting: Ishani Agarwal

Cover Design: Ronak Chavda

Price: INR 225

Printed by: booksclub.in

The opinions/ contents expressed in this book are solely of the author and do not represent the opinions/ standings/ thoughts of BookSquirrel

<u>Disclaimer</u>

This Anthology is a work of fiction. The writers have tried to make sure that all the Write-ups in this book are original, and plagiarism free.

All the write-ups in this book are unique, and they belong solely to the Co-Authors.

In case of any detection of Plagiarism, neither the publishing house, nor the compiler is to be held responsible.

The sole responsibilities of the Write-ups are on that writer.

<u>Acknowledgement</u>

The first person I would like to thank for everything, is my MOM. I don't think without your support, anything would have been possible.

My family did everything they could, to make sure I follow my passion.

Lastly, the most important thank you note goes to my Co-Authors. Had you not supported me, and helped me in this journey by being so patient, I wouldn't have been able to get this ready in such a short span of time.

<u>Co – Authors List</u>

1) Ashutosh Das (Founder - BSP)
2) Rubal Choudhary (Anthology Head - BSP)
3) Shubham Jain (Founder - Poet's Pen)
4) Ishani Agarwal (Compiler)
5) Anjana Agarwal
6) Ishika Agarwal
7) Shubham Shah
8) AshrayNasit
9) Priyadarshni Bose
10) Faheem Ul Islam
11) Sakshi Agrawal
12) Swati Kiran
13) Ishika Arora
14) Ayushi Sharma
15) Tanu Yadav
16) Aarthi Selvam
17) Riyanshi Gupta
18) Shivam Kumar
19) Pawanpreet Kaur
20) Nivedha KS
21) Aarushi Tiwari
22) Ahshaas Hussain
23) Poorvi Kumar
24) RishaJagga
25) Ananya Srivastava
26) Muskan Shah
27) Anurag Bharti
28) ShobikaBalaraman
29) Shruti Sonthalia
30) Sayandeep Patra
31) SitadeviMuthkhod
32) Mansi Jain
33) Anushka Bhati

34) Shilpa V
35) Sanjukta Raychaudhuri
36) Seemantika Das
37) Dharmraj Verma
38) Utkarsh Sharma
39) Suman Gupta
40) Alisha Kumari
41) Leena AfshaIshrot
42) Meenakshi
43) Gargi Bhattacharjee
44) AayshaSiddiqua
45) PayalLodha
46) Chitransh Srivastava
47) Rekha Abbott
48) Himanshu Rawat
49) Rishav Banerjee
50) IshantNikure
51) Vaishnavidevi
52) Priyanka Bose
53) Deepak Anantha Rao
54) Rohan Tyagi
55) Roshni Panjabi
56) Aryan Verma
57) Sukrutha B
58) Abhishek V Jaiswal

Ashutosh Das (Founder – Book Squirrel Publication)

Ashutosh Das, born on 10th Oct '98 in Bihar and brought

up in M.P and currently settled in Indore. He is pursuing

a Degree in B. Visual Arts. For him, writing is eternal

love. A writer, Author, Compiler, Storyteller, Poet, and a

performer. He is just walking and trying to make roads

for coming writers easy!

Founder of BookSquirrel Publication House

Instagram: @mr.ash.10

Rubal Choudhary (Anthology Head – Book Squirrel Publication)

This is Rubal Choudhary from Gurgaon, Haryana. She is 20-year-old and currently pursuing English Hons. from Delhi University. She aspires to become an IAS officer. She is a content writer. She has co- authored 20 Anthologies, and has Compiled 7 books in that one had won and recognized by India book of records, and The Anthology name BLACK. She is an Anthology head at BookSquirrel Publications. Earlier, writing was not a cup of tea for her but later she realized that she can write too.

<u>She - The Empowerment</u>

Women remember your power and Elegance

Remember you are love endlessly.

Remember you are the creator of your household

Remember you are the depth of blue marine.

Remember you are here for a reason.

Remember you are here to set your own limits, not to be in limits.

Remember you are not here to get trapped.

You are born to fly not to get caged.

You are born as a warrior to fight with bloodshed.

You were born with the Saccharine and pure heart.

You are born to intertwined with respect of humanity.

You are born to remove inequality and raise

economy.

You were born with an measureless soul.

You were born to name your own Destiny

Shubham Jain (Founder – Poet's Pen)

Hailing from the city of marbles & mines – Makrana (The Marble City of India), Shubham Jain is a performer. He works as a CSE in ISON Experiences, Gurgaon. Having seen his interest stoop towards poetry over the years, he set himself towards chasing his passion for writing and performing. He has been into this for quite a while now. His debut poetry book "A Way to Poetry" is slated to hit the bookshelves in the second half of the upcoming year. With this book, he delves into the highly unexplored genre of love life and poetry.

Find him on:

Instagram: @poet_shub

Gmail: sjain01ajmer@gmail.com

Ishani Agarwal (Compiler)

Ishani Agarwal here.

"You read a lot, so you have a lot of plots. Why don't you utilize it?"

These were the words Ishani's closest friend had told her.

And after much persuasion from his end, she decided to scribble, "What is the worst that can happen? People will make fun of it?" She kept telling this to herself but, her alter ego kept telling her, "I can do it. I can make it."

That's how the alter ego helped her in this journey of writing in the year of 2019.....

Born and brought up in Kolkata, she has done her schooling and college from here itself.

She is a distinguished A+ certified NCC cadet, and that as a fact is a pride statement for her.

She is doing her post graduation at the moment.

Debuting her book, with absolute lack of experience, Ishani is filled with a nervous yet exciting energy around her.

For people who do not know her, thinks she is a quiet child. But for those who do, are fed up by how much she has to talk, never getting tired.

Been a public speaker and always up for all kinds of activities in both her school and college times, she is not stage shy.

Ishani loves talking to people around, and is excited for this new beginning of hers!

Been a Compiler for 10+ Anthologies, and in the process for more, also, Coauthored 35+ Anthologies, Ishani is very Happy with how her life is turning out now!

<u>Women</u>

Yes she bleeds!
Yet, she is raped.
Yes, she is sexually attractive!
Is that the reason she isn't respected?
24*7 is the kind of duty she gives.
Be it her parents, or siblings, or in laws, or Husband, or kids, or even grandkids,
Anyone in pain, she is there to help.
No matter what happens to her, she is always there when someone needs her.
It is she, who cries in pain during childbirth,
It is she who bears the kid in her womb for 9 months,
But in the end, it is the Father's name that the child gets.
She does everything, from Dusk to dawn,
Yet, she is somehow always at fault for something or the other.
Is it her fault she is born a girl?
Why is she at fault?
You should be proud of her.
If not for her, the existence of mankind would stop.
If not for her, there would be no males either.
She is not to be raped.
Neither is she to be bargained for Dowry.
Respect her, and she will do the same.
If you don't, well, don't expect the same from her.

Anjana Agarwal

I am Anjana Agarwal.

Writing has been my way of expression since I was small. It's because writing gives me happiness.

Born n brought up in Shillong, married in Kolkata, It's through words that I portray emotions best.

Been a Co-author in 20+ Anthologies recently.

Insta handle: anjana5408

<u>Women's day do we really respect women??</u>

Think ??

In my life I have seen many ups and downs. My mom is my inspiration all throughout. From the last 50yrs, she is doing for her family. She never complained. In a very young age she got my responsibility on her head but she faced it happily and did all her chores without any complain.

In my word, this is called a perfect woman. A perfect daughter-in-law. Whether all liked or not, a perfect sister-in-law too. Whenever they were in bad times, she always helped. A perfect wife. Always beside her husband and being his best friend and support system. A perfect mother to teach children not to worry in bad times also and face and struggle no need to see behind. But, what she got in her life?? Betrayal from elders when all work was done thrown out as there is no use of her but I respect her a lot as she never looked behind and strongly believed everything will be fine.

This called a strong woman.

She never showed off like other does. As she so beautiful, smart and elegant she is a perfect woman in my life. No one can say in this world that she has done anything bad for anyone.

Ishika Agarwal

Ishika Agarwal.

Being a class 10th student, my imagination ran wild. I tried penning down my imaginations.

Love Writing. It is nothing else but a passion.

From Kolkata.

Also, into extra-curricular activities!

Been a Co-author in 20+ anthologies in the recent past.

Insta handle: ishika_agarwal13

<u>Women</u>

Respect them

You will get whatever you want.

Respect them

They will fulfill all your wishes.

Respect them

And you will never get hurt.

If you dare disrespect them

They can finish you.

****

Women

Love them,

Care for them,

Respect them,

As they are very special people

Cause without them we would not be there.

Shubham Shah

Shubham Shah, entrepreneur at "Flairs & Glairs" a brand with dynamics in events organizing and cultural educational pan INDIA.

He has initiated with his own open mic platform to help budding poets and aspiring writers under his brand named as **"Teekhe Zasbaaat"**

He says Writing has impersonated him since childhood and he has now been writing for over a decade!

Cooking, on the other hand, is his passion!

He also mentions, trying out new things just tickles him!

He adds, "agar jasbaat teekhe na ho toh wo jasbaat kaha" Spices are all that blends! So do his words!

As a chef, he presents to you his dish! Hot and freshly served! Taste it! Feel it! Enjoy it!

With his passion to explore opportunities across Platforms he is working with keen devotion and we wish him all the very best for his future ventures

Share your reviews on his

INSTAGRAM handle -@spicy_emotions / @shubham4shah

Or via email on - shubham2shah@gmail.com

<u>Diamond</u>

She is hard as diamond. She shines like a diamond. She is precious like a diamond. She is a woman, a girl, a sister, a friend, a wife, a mother, and a daughter.

Can you name one incident where you can just fit in without her by your side? Unfortunately, No! Even if that's possible without her efforts just take a pause to think twice. Would you even be born if she wasn't there? Then why do we as a male put in the so called "Male Ego" or rather where it comes from? One substantial fact that I eventually learnt in life is, its fine if you admit to have stood a step behind a lady! She is a Leader there's no shame in following her.

Do we as males stand equality against the one who gave us omnipresent in one or the other form? Oh! Did I just mention **Omnipresent!** Isn't that what being the almighty is? Yes! I agree to the fact that the concept of being a feminist comes into picture, but it would be my request for your thought to have it googled first. **Equality is the true feminism!**

Yes, I praise my lady for every little success I attain. Every single fortune I happen to taste and I truly feel proud every night to have thanked her for her efforts. She is arrogant, she is reluctant, she is adamant! But she isn't Ignorant.

She stands by me, even when in anger. She refuses to accept but she truly admires the way I seek to have her! She is love! She is life! She is my pride!

Lakshmi is what I call her! Since the day she walked in, I tasted fortune, I tasted gradual success. Yes, with her footprints, the course of my action was directed to positivity! Every day one after the other I feel something filling in and something changing like someone is constantly burning my hard disk by over writing the obsolete and corrupt data! Yes! I am changing for good and it's just because of this one lady!

Thank You Miss_tbh, for your efforts.

Thank you for being there.

Ashray Nasit

Ashray Nasit is 20 years old and living in Gujarat. As he is a Biotechnologist and a singer, he believes in making of better science by use of various arts. He is a fond of Indian Classical music and Ancient Sanskrit Literature, as well as Indian tradition and philosophy. Being a Reiki and Crystal healing practitioner, he believes that every outcomes reflected from his personality are the desired results of the cosmic energy, which leads his heart to the narration of various shades of feelings by Words. His motto is that the way to his goal begins from his own soul. (You can write to him at ashray84252@gmail.com)

तू नारी !

सृष्टि के सर्जन का साज है नारी !
रब की ख्वाहिशो का वजूद है नारी !
सुनी पड़ी थी जब दुनिया सारी,
विधाता ने बनाई तब नारी जाति !

सर्जनहार का करिश्मा नारी !
देवी स्वरूपा तू बागबानी !
हर गुणों को समाए बैठी,
जग में है तू सबसे न्यारी !

वात्सल्य का उपवन तू नारी !
प्रेम का तू परचम नारी !
शक्ति की शाश्वतता वाली,
धरती की धड़कन तू नारी !

संस्कृति की शान तू नारी !
रागिणी तू वंदना की !
ममता की मजधार तू नारी,
महिमा अपरंपार तिहारी !

Priyadarshni Bose

Priyadarshni Bose from Odisha is a Science student likes to write short social poems. She is interested in doing so because she wants to create awareness among the society.

She never believes in what we are rather believe in what we will be…

<u>नारी का रूप</u>

तू नारी है तो सनमान है,
तू बहन है तो हिम्मत हैं,
तू बिवी है तो चाहत हैं,
तू बहू है तो मान हैं,
तू बेटी है तो रहमत हैं,
अंत मे सबसे खास,
तू माँ है तो पूरी जन्नत हैं।

Faheem Ul Islam

Faheem ul islam hails from Achanpulwama, Jammu and Kashmir pursuing my bachelor's Honors in political science at ALIGARH MUSLIM UNIVERSITY. Aim to become HUMAN RIGHT ACTIVIST to be the voice of voiceless people.
My Dad is inspiration for all this.♥☐

Instagram id: faheem_smile
Whatsapp number: 8006662640

<u>EVERYDAY IS WOMEN'S DAY</u>

A woman is so much more than just a human being. She has Gods power to create a life, to cope with so much pain and somehow always end up being the strongest one in every room. But nowadays, Women is the word which we see by disgraceful eyes in the contemporary world because we have been dominated by west where there is no distinguished word of mother, sister and wife. The present day our society is turning towards all these types of deeds where we are being bounded by inferiority complex. The same situation today was happening in Pre_Arabia where the women was treated nothing but a toy used for one's lust. But then the only holy way of life and complete guidance for human beings (ISLAM) lift up the miserable condition of this pity creature. And it got a high and reputed status in the society. The creature which was being treated as nothing much as animals, Islam gives her full rights and Islam teaches us when a girl takes birth in a house it is blessings from god, and when this girl grown up and attain the age of marriage it completes the half Eeman of her husband and when this women becomes mother the paradise lies beneath her feet. This is the status of women. There is no such a special day where we will remember these women as sister, wife, mother but the whole year is dedicated to this creature because we all are just because of this creature. Behind every successful person there is a big hand of women. And if a woman understands the problems of house in the near future she will understand the problems of country. So as per my own views the women is strength of a person as a sister, wife and mother. We should respect them at every stage as being the brother we should be the bodyguards of our sisters, we should love them and should make a pious bond where a sister can feel the safest. And when we get married we should love her with all our efforts because she is also a human being; she has a heart and a women loves her husband much more than others. The mother which loves us at every stage we should also take care of her and love her. So we should pay attention towards this all and love this creature.

Sakshi Agrawal

She is SAKSHI AGRAWAL. She is from Muzaffarpur, Bihar. She is just 17 year old, A little realistic, and a lot poetic. She is just in the way to make her father feel proud. She is a great dreamer, just try to pen down whatever comes in her heart. She says writing is her soul's deepest passion.

Women We built a fort around you, Behind the walls of words, Wild, Charming, graceful, motherly, A chain you got used to, Forgot you could break free Like the elephant chained from being a calf forgets to use his strength to break free. Now, a whirlpool of shame, dishonor, abuse.... Tries to suck you in a conspiracy of the dispossessed and threatened. Remember, the world is more than ever in need of you for your strength, intelligence, preservance, imagination... In its crisis. Let's give a Clarion's call for a human world, not a man made world.

Swati Kiran

Hello! I am Swati from BIHAR, INDIA. An ambitious woman who is here to make her mother proud. I love to spread happiness and positivity all around myself. Also, I run a charitable trust of mine named "Rintej Foundation" with a motto "Serving, Sharing and Caring".

लड़की हूं कमज़ोर नहीं

ख़ामोश हूँ, बेज़ुबान नहीं
इंसान हूँ, कोई चीज़ नहीं.
तुम रोक सको,
वो हवा से पलटता पन्ना नहीं,
हाँ मैं लड़की हूँ, कमज़ोर नहीं.

तुम गालियाँ दो, मैं सहती जाऊँ
कोई काठ की बनी गुड़िया नहीं.
लड़ूँगी, गिरूँगी और फिर ऊठूँगी
हारके बैठ जाऊँ,
मैं इतनी भी बुज़दिल नहीं.
हाँ मैं लड़की हूँ, कमज़ोर नहीं.

तुम हाथ लगाओ, तो मैं डर जाऊँ
कोई पानी की मैं मछली नहीं.
दुर्गा और काली मैं बन जाऊँ,
तुमसे डरने वाली कोई बच्ची नहीं.
हाँ मैं लड़की हूँ, कमज़ोर नहीं.

अरे, कभी तो तुम इंसानियत सीख जाओ,
हैवानों जैसी ये ज़िन्दगी तुम्हारी अच्छी नहीं.
और अब हमें तुम चुप करवा दो,
तुम्हारी इतनी हस्ती नहीं.

हाँ मैं लड़की हूँ, कमज़ोर नहीं.

बेटी हूँ मैं, खिलौना नहीं
माँ हूँ मैं, माल नहीं
तुम मिटा दो, वो कच्ची स्याही नहीं.
हाँ मैं लड़की हूँ, कमज़ोर नहीं.

Ishika Arora

She is Ishika Arora. She is the founder of "The word's squad", writing is her passion. Hearts are meant to be broken. So, she started playing with the words. She is a published author, and has her two compiled anthologies.

She is not the one to be judged by from her neck to her thigh. She is not the one to be judged by Black is love till it's not a colour. Stop judging the book just by a cover. You should be tall, you are too short. If fat, they shout aunty. If thin, then too skinny. If perfect, then not beautiful, you are hot. You had to be so much prettier. You just folded up your hair. Are you sure, you will eat cheese, Try salad. Oh! Your skirt is too short for men to stare. Oh! Your kurta is too tight for men to look there. Was the allegations right the country imposed, was it Priyanka's fault to be an independent and bold. A family lost her daughter; Can we just imagine a little bit, what that girl has faced and what their family is still facing? If we can understand and stand one, No girl will go through the unbearable pain. Oo society! Stop tolerating criminals. Stop playing blame games. Let me tell you all we wear makeup and dresses to make us glad. Why to taunt, why to point, and make us sad. Nirbhaya's soul can never rest in peace seeing the criminals, justifying for their deeds. We can blame dress. We can blame time. Why can't we blame the devils and their creepy minds? Every relative says to our parents "What kind of clothes she is wearing? Short dress, crop top, etc. She is now of 16 make her wear salwar kameez, don't you know what kind of era it is?" I want to say all the relatives a single line, "Aunty agar apki bhi beti Hoti toh aaj aap Kisi ki beti ko baatein naa krti". At last, I wanna say from the colour of skin Dusky to fair, you keep on judging us everywhere. Oh! She is so tall we won't get a man. Oh! She's too short we won't get a man. STOP! STOP judging us on everywhere you find, it's not in our dress; it's in your mind.

Ayushi Sharma

Ayushi Sharma is pursuing B.Tech by profession. She is an enthusiastic writer for being passionate about calligraphy and the art of expressing words. For so long, she is a thoughts holder by raising her voice towards wrong in front of her country 'India' so proudly. An athlete also grasps her pictures in the mind of shades of a brave woman.

"World by women" She also invented the circulars of designing the power of love more than the money by her Grace and unconditional love given to family instead of receiving luxury life. Women from around the world are expected to get more respect even than an Eve teasing… A woman not actually, the strongest women who feels deeply for every single creature in her essence of being soft roses. Her tears flow just as abundantly as her laughter for being the smooth and strongest.

Tanu Yadav

She is doing engineering in computer science & lives in Bhopal, Madhya Pradesh.

A woman can't say no to a man. How can she do it, It is wrong, isn't it?? A woman doesn't have self respect, how can she refuse a man? At any cost she has to say yes to any proposal... If she says yes to every asked questions then she is the best woman, a respectable woman, she is all yours, and she is may be your girlfriend, best friend, life partner blah blah... If... if... she says "no" to a person.. Hey first of all, come on a woman doesn't have right but in the rare of the rarest situation she says "NO" ... Then suddenly she becomes a dirty woman, a whore, a slut and more... Come on... You know it's all about copyright A women is all about copyright If she is a daughter... then parents has copyright (which is harmless). If she is a girlfriend, then her boyfriend has copyright emotionally, physically, mentally... How can she say no to his boyfriend ...come on he is her boyfriend he has all rights to do anything with her without her permission because she said one more time yes to his proposal .. No she doesn't have right to say no.. If she says then she becomes an abusive thing for whole the world. Let's suppose she is single and a man proposes her and she said no to this man. We all are having ego and it hurts. How can she hurt a man ego? How can she say no to man? Suddenly, she is no more his crush or attractions... Now she becomes a slut or blah blaahh... A wife who doesn't have her name.. Hey! "Mrs. Kapoor, how are you?" always plays a best role. As a mother she washes clothes, she cleans houses, she cooks, she is one in the entire house who doesn't know about herself ...and she can't say no to his husband ...how can she do that? Come on she is married ..How can she say no to her husband. A women is the most beautiful creation of God ..We can't even imagine out world without her love and support. Where a man is the Pillar of this beautiful world. We all are same .. You are man I respect that Kindly respect my "no" No means no Now it's time to say no to world. Don't celebrate us (as women's day). Kindly respect our "No".

Aarthi Selvam

I am Aarthi Selvam an enigmatic writer in love with words and emotions. I live in the heart of Tamilnadu -Chennai Get connected with me in Instagram: enigmaticpoetess Email:aarthiselvam12@gmail.com

Being a girl she never needs to prioritize the search for her life's purpose because she was the chosen shrine designed for the souls to attain its divinity.

No woman wants to hate her own gender for the role of a victim she is been pushed into for nothing she did but just was born in this world.

Riyanshi Gupta

She is a girl full of creativity and emotions. She loves to listen to music, plays instruments like Congo.

I'm the brown daughter of a white woman who voted blue and now has made a nest called sorrow from twigs of left- wing shame, from shards of blue glass bottles and jellyfish, from coral reef blue and eye bruise blue, from her there's plenty of room for you blue, but how do I tell her I can't live there too? How do I tell her she named me after papaya flesh and cornhusk, after sweet juice of black women's song, whose only known border is water, who dip sacramental bread in Obea chant? Slow churned memories of the Arawak. Did she know they were a poetic people when she named me? Did she prophecy the sap of Ackee tree lingering in the ashen grooves of my knees and elbows? Their jerk and rock-steady lilt. What I don't know of them is the white space of every page I've not yet written. What I don't know of my people is their name.

Shivam Kumar

An 18 years old excellent communicator who is ambitious and driven. A prolific poetic person and a wild writer that wills weirdly. Writing is like an inseparable part of me.

<u>दो बातें माँ के साथ</u>

माँ तू तो कहती थी तेरा राजा बेटा हूँ मैं फिर उसने क्यों फकीर
बोल मुझे ठुकरा दिया,
माँ तू तो कहती थी अनमोल हूँ मैं फिर उसने इतनी आसानी से
कैसे मुझे भुला दिया..

माँ तू तो कहती थी तेरा शेर बेटा हूँ मैं फिर क्यों जाने से उसके
मेरे आंखों से इतने आंसू बहे,
माँ तू तो कहती थी एक खरोच तक ना आने देगी तू मुझे तो फिर
क्यों मैंने बिन चोट के इतने दर्द सहे..

हाँ मानता हूँ माँ की मेरा पहला प्यार तू है पर न जाने दूसरा वह
कब और कैसे हो गई,
माँ प्यार तो मैंने उसकी अच्छाई और नेकी देखकर की थी न जाने
कब वो वैसी हो गई..

माँ तूने तो आज तक गिरने ना दिया मुझे उसने मुझे खुद की ही
नजरों में गिरने को मजबूर कर दिया,
माँ तू तो कहती थी तेरे बेटे का दिल बड़ा मज़बूत है पर माँ उसने
पल भर में ही चकनाचूर कर दिया..

माँ तू तो मेरे नाराज होने पर मुझ को ही मनाया करती थी ना
फिर वह क्यों मुझसे नजरें चुरा कर भाग गई,

माँ तूने तो आज तक सबसे मीठे बोलने को ही सिखाया था ना फिर वह क्यों कड़वे बोल के बाण दाग गई..

माँ तूने तो उंगली पकड़ चलना सिखाया था ना उसने भरे दलदल में मुझको ढकेल दिया,
माँ तूने तो दुनिया भर की बुराइयों से बचाया था ना फिर उसने क्यों पलभर में ही उनके बीच ठेल दिया..

माँ तू तो बारिश पड़ने पर भी अपने आंचल का सहारा दिया करती थी ना उसने क्यों मुझको आंधियों के बीच अकेला छोड़ दिया,
माँ तूने तो हमेशा नदियों के किनारे संजोकर रखा था ना फिर उसने क्यों दरिया के बीच छोड़कर मुझको मुझ से मुंह मोड़ लिया..।

Pawanpreet Kaur

Pawanpreet Kaur is a girl who believes that a pen is her best-friend which helps her relieving the stress by penning her life stories into words. Since childhood, she loves Reading and collecting articles from newspapers and magazines. She has a flair for writing, which she discovered when she was 16 years old and she started penning a poem for her niece. Since then she started writing. Then she got a chance to get published in an anthology for the first time when she was 19 years old. She is also very fond of art and craft as well as writing. Till now she worked as a Co-Author in so many Anthologies and many of them are coming soon. Now she is also working as a compiler.

<u>Be Strong</u>

This is the message to all those people who don't wanna be in this world anymore because of their breakup or any other reason. Be Strong as a girl who bleeds 7 days in a month without having any wounds with a lot of pain and still manages to live. Be strong as a girl who got harassed a lot of times in a single day but still manages to live. Be strong as a girl who is tortured by her husband or boyfriend but still manages to live. Be strong as a girl who get raped and still manages to live and start her new life. Do you really think that you don't want to be in this world anymore? Think again.

Nivedha KS

I am Nivedha.K.S, pursuing B.A. English Literature under the institution 'Sri GVG Visalakshi College for Women'. An aspiring writer, who is always enthralled by the beauty of the nature and is hoping to induce a 'True Sense of Literature'. Occasionally, I come up with some piece of poetry and have started to publish them. I'm thankful for my parents and friends, who have constantly encouraged me in identifying my hidden talents.

<u>**My Unwearied Women:**</u>

Oh! My Unwearied Women,
Why don't ye rest for a while,
When thine journey is always 'run a mile'.
You have to undergo an inimical exile,
In order to maintain your strong profile.
You enter into an unknown house as 'one hired',
Yet,
After all your constant efforts, thee known as 'one dried'.
Some alienate you due to your 'off style',
Though you win them back with your warm smile.

Oh! My Unwearied Women,
Why don't ye rest for a while,
When thine journey is always ' run a mile'.
You keep on moving ahead like a Nile,
Though your work bundles up like a pile.
You always spread your love like a fire,
Yet you will be the one left in a mire.
Now,
It is the time to wind-up these stuffs for awhile,
And travel towards the one thee always aspire.

Aarushi Tiwari

I'm Aarushi Tiwari. Raw yet passionate writer. I owe my everything to my parents Mrs. Sunita Tiwari and Mr. Anil Kumar Tiwari.

<u>Creature with Honour</u>

Women are a symphony,
Endowed with numerous
And unimaginable traits.
Spreading love, peace and harmony!

Her essence lies,
in her patience.
Taking the highest flight,
Soaring in the sky like a kite,
She'll put efforts to bring you to light.

You might shoot her with words,
She'll go through everything.
Bearing allegations every now and then,
That are way too absurd.
Yet she'll smile without whining about.

Approach to her,
with right mindset.
Ain't your liability,
Rather an asset!

A tender yet valorous creature she is -
Will be the mistress of all oddities.
Whether the day be sunny or covered
with mist...making no fuss
(will) Manage to work from dawn to dusk.
Giving you just a gist -
Treat her as a Goddess,
Even though you're an atheist!!

Ahshaas Hussain

Ahshaas Hussain hails from Sambalpur, Odisha. He is a post-graduate student of Gangadhar Meher University in English. He is the co-author of 15+ Anthologies. He is an ardent lover of Humanism and English Literature. He believes in universal approaches of Magic.

<u>Women by Ahshaas Hussain</u>

Hurricanes
Tornadoes
Tsunamis
Volcanic eruptions
Woman

Strong
Fierce
And beautiful too

Nothing is stronger
Than her trying to
Build herself again
Strong as the winds
Fierce as the lava
Beautiful as the high waves

The word "woman" in itself is so
unfathomably strong
That at times she forgets her worth
She's shines brighter than diamonds

What could be more glorious than this?

To be as strong as force of nature
To be wild
To be of your own
To own yourself without
any guilt or regret

Embrace the glorious
mess that you are
Love your freckles
Love your thighs

Love yourself
Start with yourself
Become what you dreamt of
Empower women

Be a force that people love to look at you work

Build castles when they throw bricks at you

Go fierce for a while and then forever
Leave a mark in their heads

For hurricanes and earthquakes
weren't just named after
woman like that.

Poorvi Kumar

A girl of small town, Poorvi, have big dreams in her eyes and putting forward her each step to fulfill those dreams. She is a student of class 12. Despite being the daughter of a business man, Poorvi lives to write and express herself through words. She loves to play with words and convey her thoughts to others. She had spent her 14 years in St. Basil's School, where she has learnt a lot. Her only aim is to make her parents feel proud of her.

स्त्री है तू

दुर्गा भी तू , लक्ष्मी भी तू ,
मां सरस्वती का रूप भी तू ,
संकट में काली बन जाए ,
ममता की मूरत , पार्वती भी तू ।

ना किसी से कम है तू,
ना ही कोई तेरे समान ,
सृष्टि का संचार है तुझसे,
ए स्त्री तू सबसे महान ।

पानी का बहाव हो तुम,
मां गंगा का स्वरूप,
धरती मां का आभार हो तुम,
हमारे पापों का नाश हो तुम ।

जिम्मेदारियों को बखूबी निभाती हो ,
घर हो या दफ्तर, हर जगह संतुलन बनाती हो,
सुन्दरता की मूरत हो तुम,
जैसी भी हो, बहुत खूबसूरत हो तुम ।

अपनी कमज़ोरियों को अपनी ताकत बना लेती हो ,
जहां जाती हो सबका मन मोह लेती हो ,
समानता की परिभाषा हो तुम ,
आज़ादी की किरण हो तुम ।

Risha Jagga

Risha Jagga D/o Mr. OM PRAKASH JAGGA Silence lover but a rising voice, she is full of grace. Often caught with a cup of tea and a notepad in pocket. Moulding emotions and feelings of others by deep observation in her hobby. Sometimes overthinking kill us inside but she is the one who can make you happy. She has participated in more than 42 Anthologies. You can read her quotes on Instagram @diary_of_love_pain_

My hands are shivering
I'm afraid
He is still outside the cage
Drunk and shouting outside my gate
I m feeling like a victim again.

8 months nothing changed
The day I found I am happy
Is the day I cry on that same day
No one is there to hug me and say it wasn't your mistake.

I can't cry my heart is afraid
Afraid again of loosing myself
And got into that depression phase
I have to show them that I am normal
Even if I am dying.

I am a girl who is always being taught
Taught how to behave who to show emotions and how to fake.
I can't even cry in my own nest where I took birth.
I am just another responsibility I don't have emotions I am just
another puppet.

I am just another girl, dying inside but smiling in front of my dear
society.

Ananya Shrivastav

Hey this is Ananya Shrivastav from Basti, Uttar Pradesh. I'm still studying in class 11th but my hobby is writing and I think so that it would take me to some special place I'm belonging from, very undeveloped city few of them knows about it.

Women, She is the real beauty she works for nothing, she is not stronger than you not powerful than you but what she can do you can't even think in your dreams. She is not free like you, but you know what, she has the most beautiful soul and nothing can break her confidence. She's main weakness is her family but if once her mind turned off, no one can save you. Mostly women are called goddess Laxmi but she will be goddess Mahakaali if it comes to her family or her own self, never think that women are still at 2nd place because now it's just proverbs that women's can't do anything, once in a time let her fly she will show you the real feel of air, once in a time let her run she will show you the real feel of soil, once in a life let her move on she will show you the real good vibes. Respect her like no one can because she is real women not your slave, real women should be the strongest not to be weakest.

Muskan Shah

An amateur writer, A CS aspirant, still working on her dreams. This 20 year old girl hails from Jharsuguda a small town in Odisha. She has been a part of 10+ Anthologies till date and compiler of two.

<u>नारी के रूप</u>

वो दुर्गा भी है,

वो काली भी है,

वो पावन सी झिलमिल,

सवाली भी है,

वो है पार्वती,

वो लक्ष्मी भी है,

वो बहती अपनी धुन में,

एक झील भी है,

वो सरस्वती,

वो गौरी,

वो कांटो में सजी,

एक फूल सी है,

वो औरत इस जहां में,

मिसाल वो मानो किल सी है,

दबे तो दब जाए अपनो के खातिर,

पर चुभे तो हो जाए दर्द भी जाहिर,

वो समय आने पर,

साधन भी है,

वो समझने में कुछ,

मुश्किल भी है,

वो है तो इस जहां में,

रंगीनियां सी है,

वो ना हो तो,

कहां कोई कहानियां सी है,

वो औरत जरूरत हर घर की,

वो नारी मूरत शांत शील सी है।।

Anurag Bharti

Anurag Bharti, is a graduation student from Darbhanga, Bihar. He is interested in poem and story writing and also loves singing. He was born on 25 August 1999.

वो शक्तिशाली है दुर्गा है काली है वो औरत है जो कभी ना झुकने वाली है वो मुश्किलों से लड़ने वाली है वो हर धर्य रखने वाली है वो औरत है जो हर कदम पे साथ चलने वाली है वो करुणा दया की देवी है जो सबको समझने वाली है वो औरत है जो माफ करने वाली है वो पवित्र है वो श्रद्धा है वो जल की शीतलता है वो औरत है जो अग्नि की ज्वाला है वो आशीर्वाद है वो भगवान का दिया एक वरदान है वो औरत है जो अंधेरे में जलती एक मशाल है वो धर्म है वो खुदा की इबादत है वो औरत है जो बरसती हुई सावन की पहली बरसात है

****

एक औरत ने मुझे जन्म दिया एक औरत ने मुझे इस दुनियाँ में जिने के काबिल बनाया। एक औरत ने मुझे हर मुश्किल में मेरा साथ दिया एक औरत ने मुझे प्रेम किया। एक औरत ने मुझे भाई का दर्जा दिया एक औरत ने मुझे पति का दर्जा दिया। एक औरत ने मुझे मर्द होने का गौरव प्रदान किया एक औरत ने मुझे नाम दिया। एक औरत ने मुझे पूरा किया एक औरत ने मुझे जीवन जीने का लक्ष्य दिया। एक औरत ने मुझे मेरा अस्तित्व दिया एक औरत ने मुझे अपने मान सम्मान के रक्षक होने का अवसर दिया।

Shobika Balaraman

Shobika Balaraman is an aspiring bard and writer. She, an adorable daughter is ardent in writing treatises and poems. She hails from Udumalpet, an alluring town from where she is pursuing her UG 3rd year in English Literature at Sri GVG Visalakshi College for Women.

<u>O' Ye Women!</u>

O' ye the blithe of green!
Thou turn the world an emerald sheen,
And bloom in eminent
Coz of thine pure scent;

O' ye the sturdy of mellow!
Thou turn the world a hallow,
And instill the dawn
Coz not to down;

O' ye the amour of red!
Thou turn the world a steed,
And procure a meed
Coz of thy gallant deed;

O' ye the dawn of light,
Thou turn the world to knight,
And preach them delight
Coz of thine keen sight;

O' ye the dusk of dark,
Thou turn the world embark,
And hold in stark
Coz of thy holy spark.

Shruti Sonthalia

"Follow your dreams and your heart! "My motto for life is simple. My dream is to succeed in the fashion industry (as professionally I am a fashion designer) and my heart has the passion for writing. Feelings often find expression in terms of poetry and that gives me the fervor to work hard. If I could make a difference to one life around me it would make me feel happy. This poem in particular is an attempt to change the frame of mind of women towards men folk. Love and respect is what we want and that is what we women want to share.

<u>Wo-MAN</u>

Someone wished me

#Happy_Woman's #Day!!!

नारी तुम प्रेम हो,आस्था हो विश्वास हो,
टूटी हुई उम्मीदों की एक मात्र आस हो ..

हर जान का तुम ही तो आधार हो
नफरत की दुनिया में तुम ही प्यार हो ..

उठो अपने अस्तित्व को संभालो
केवल एक दिन ही नहीं,
हर दिन के लिए तुम खास हो...

और मैंने उनसे कहाँ..........

प्रेम हमारा अधूरा है जब तक ना आपका एहसास हो ,
हम आपकी आस्था है यह हमें विश्वास हो ।
हमारी उम्मीद सिर्फ़ आप से है ;
आप ही हमारी आस हो ।
हमारी जान आप में अटकी है क्यूँकि आप ही हमारा प्यार हो ,
हर दिन अपने दिल को सम्भाले हुए है क्यूँकि इसमें सिर्फ़ आप हो
!
हमारा अस्तित्व आप से है , हमें आप पे गर्व है ....

आपको हमारा बस ख़याल रहे - यह उस उम्मीद का पर्व है।

A man and woman complement each other and we shall not compete!!

Sayandeep Patra

A boy from a small town is studying engineering and an entrepreneur. Always had a dream of becoming a writer is presently heading forward to fulfill it.

Fe: - Iron
 Male :- man
That is why we say that every man is an Ironman (Tony Stark) only when there is a Pepper Potts with him. I wish every woman including my motherland a very Happy International Woman's Day.

Sitadevi Muthkhod

Meet our co-author Sitadevi Muthkhod (pen-name: siyahi), currently a CSE undergraduate from Mumbai. Sita has a strong inclination towards English and Hindi literature. Her work has been published in several anthologies. Sita writes on various topics, but is an aduler of the sun. She often weaves poems based on stories of her commute friends. She credits her sisters and her friend for being her constant motivation. She also runs at marathons and volunteers for social causes. A budding poet, Sita is eager to explore and develop her writing skills. She can be reached on social media handles.

Not yet, but I'll go, I'll go
To be the radiant moon
And set up my light show
Not tonight, but very soon

When the sun stops overshadowing me
With his blinding rays of light
I smell the whiff of jealousy
When the earthlings still crave for my sight

When they're filled with nostalgia
With broken hearts and despair
To me they call out, oh Cynthia!
'Cause they know I'm always there

They bare themselves to me with trust
Through soundproof walls I hear them scream
They speak to me of love and lust
They speak to me of their shattered dream

During the day they get things done
The world they create is pristine
But it is to me that they run
To seek the beauty feminine

I borrow your light, I agree
To make myself visible at night
Even the blind wombs can feel me
We both are nurturers, we need not fight

Mansi Jain

Mansi Jain is a 17 year old young writer from commerce background. She is writing poems since the past 3 years. She likes to put her feelings on paper through poetry. Through her poetry she delivers all her life experiences and events that she comes through in her daily life.

<u>YOU GOTTA UNDERSTAND'</u>

You need therapy
I don't say that mockingly
But when you defend the man
And discredit the women
When you listen to his history
And ignore hers
When you say "but they are such good boys"
And then say "she should have known better"
You need a therapist
To become your exorcist
You need help to purge the misogyny
You've been fed you all life
The Misogyny
That tells you are small
You are voiceless
You are meant for men and not for yourself
The misogyny
That tells you- you to become only a wife
And not a warrior
The misogyny
That tells you the
Default in believing him
And not believing her.

Anushka Bhati

I am Anushka Bhati from Ajmer, Rajasthan. I am 16 years old and a budding writer. Writing and public speaking are my passion and I aspire to become a journalist. Instagram @suroor_e_shayari

<u>नारी</u>

हर नारी यज्ञसेनी सी पवित्र है,

लांछन ना लगाना यूँ उसके चरित्र पे।

अग्नि है हर स्त्री के व्यक्तित्व में,

प्रश्नचिह्न ना लगाना यूँ उसके अस्तित्व पे।

शिखा में उसकी लपटें है, नैनो में अंगारे हैं।

नारी अपमान की पात्र नही, उसके कदमों में सितारे है।

एक हाथ में वात्सल्य समेटे, दूजे में शस्त्र संभाले है।

बदन में सूर्य की किरणें हैं जो बुरी नज़र को जलाये है।

न जला ज्योति उसमे प्रतिशोध की,

प्रचंड है ज्वाला उसके क्रोध की।

उसकी शक्ति का तुझे बोध नहीं,

दुष्टों के संघार का उसे अफसोस नहीं।

महाभारत का इतिहास दोहराया जाएगा,

इस युग में भी हर दुष्कर्मी मारा जाएगा।

Shilpa V

Shilpa Veeramani hails from Udumalpet, Tamilnadu. She is pursuing BA English literature. She is a passionate writer and a poetess. Her interest in writing lead her to her web novel "Meant to be" and her site's address is shilpasrecitals.com. She owes her success to her Appa and Amma.

<u>Complement of Men</u>

Ye women thee art the compliment of men-

But thy grace is not what men summon.

Thy visage hath neurons of amazement,

But why are they intimidated by just thy body?

Why doth they ruin your scared body,

Whilst they also worship thy as their "Goddess"?

Why thee art the second sex,

Whilst they are given life from you?

Why doth they crush thy crimson heart,

With their privilege of marriage?

Why do thee still remain silent,

When they proudly entitle themselves as Millennials,

Why doth thee not claiming your throne,

For thee are the compliments of men,

Without whom they can't survive!

Sanjukta Raychaudhuri

Sanjukta Raychaudhuri is an Electrical and Electronics Engineer, residing in Hyderabad. When she isn't glued to the computer screen at work, she spends her time reading, cooking and tries hard not to binge watch a new series. She also maintains a small library in her house.

<u>Who is she?</u>

She's a confidante, a home economist, a best friend.

She's a mother. She's a woman.

She's a partner in crime, a guardian angel, a critic.

She's a sister. She's a woman.

She's an unpaid therapist, an extended family.

She's a friend. She's a woman.

She's a companion, a human sanctuary.

She's a wife. She's a woman.

She sacrifices her desires,

She prioritizes everyone except herself,

She endures monthly ache without complaints,

She undergoes excruciating pain during labour,

She maintains the balance between work and home,

She is a force to reckon with,

She is a woman.

Seemantika Das

SEEMANTIKA.. An English Lecturer by profession and a fervent art lover at heart. She loves to Dance, sing, Paint, write, Speak and to do all such things which involves living LIFE. A long training in NCC and Sports has taught her to be confident, fearless and to have a positive attitude. A trained Odissi and Sambalpuri folk dancer, she is a Doordarshan and AIR approved Anchor too. Her family being her strongest support, she draws her inspiration from the positivity around her.

WOMAN..YOU ARE STRONG !!!

Have you ever seen
A tired body
Wobbly legs
Shaking hands
Tearful and sleepy eyes
Irritated mind…
Cooking food for a family, Nourishing a family
That's a WOMAN, working tirelessly everyday…

How can we ever measure the amount of hard work she puts in…?
The sleepless nights...
The heart wrenching sacrifices...
The unconditional love that she pours in...

You are definitely STRONG...Woman!!
But hey
Slow down when you are tired
Stop when you are unheard
Question when you are not responded
Protest when you are burdened...
And it's OK when you do so
Learn to say NO when you feel so...

Just remember to accept yourself the way you are...
Let us muster up the courage to stand by each other
Let us be each other's strength…
Let us put our HAPPINESS on the priority list this time...
Let us LIVE our own Life without feeling Guilty
And No, you are not selfish when you do so…

Yes WOMAN...YOU ARE STRONG
Strong enough to say that...
We don't need a single day in the Calendar to celebrate
WOMANHOOD…
As we celebrate LIFE itself every day,
In each and every moment...

Dharmraj Verma

Myself DHARMRAJ VERMA, Resident of Tonk, Rajasthan. Currently, I am pursuing MBBS from AIIMS Rishikesh.

<u>क़ाफ़िला बड़ा हुआ तो क्या.........</u>

बड़ा काफ़िला हुआ तो क्या, उठा पैर तू चल वहाँ...

ढूँढ अपनी लौ को तू, जहाँ जले वो चल वहाँ...

जला चिंगारी तू रूह से, लड़खड़ाना बस छोड़ दे....

आँख पड़ी तुझपे घूरकर, तू उस नज़र को मोड़ दे...

कर कोशिश तू लाख दफ़ा, नूर तेरा तू ख़ुद का यहाँ....

बड़ा काफ़िला हुआ तो क्या, उठा पैर तू चल वहाँ 2

शाम हुई तो क्या हुआ, नशा रात का भर ज़रा...

ढूँढ ख़ुद को तू वहाँ, दिन नही अब हरा भरा....

मशाल ख़ुद की जला ले तू, दिनकर तू अब यहाँ वहाँ...

देख ख़ुद को सूरज में डूबो कर, आग तेरी नही कहाँ कहाँ....

बड़ा काफ़िला हुआ तो क्या, उठा पैर तू चल वहाँ.....2

मन की बेड़ियों को तोड़ ज़रा , उन्मुक्त ख़ुद को मान ले...

बुनियाद गढ़ ले सपनों की, सच को साझा जान ले...

मढ़ ले ख़ुद को सख़्त बन, बन जा तू एक प्रगाढ़ बला...

सन्तोष से तू कोमल रह ,हैं माधुर्य में सब घात भला ....

सुकूं अपने आप को दे ज़रा, बना कठोर तू तेरा जहाँ....

बड़ा काफ़िला हुआ तो क्या, उठा पैर तू चल वहाँ...... 2

मूँद नही तू अब आँखों को, नैन पूरे खोल ले....

देख साहिल ख़ुद का तू, निडर तू ख़ुद को बोल ले...

जो आते नापाक तेरे बीच में, वहीं तू उनको दफ़ना दे..

रख पापियो की हरकत पे खंजर, तू औरत परिचय अपना दे...

करले ख़ुद से प्यार ज़रा, रोने को तू अब चली कहाँ...

बड़ा काफ़िला हुआ तो क्या, उठा पैर तू चल वहाँ.... 2

सपनों की मंज़िल ढूँढ ले,आँखों में भर ले ख़्वाब बड़े...

अकस्मात् टूट के नही बिखरना, काँटे आगे हैं गडे पड़े....

ख़ुद का अस्तित्त्व लाना हैं, औरत मूल को मधुर बनाना हैं.....

लाचार मानना ख़ुद को तू बस छोड़ दे, भव्य सौम्यता को जाना हैं...

तेरा पैमाना हैं विशाल बड़ा, प्रत्यक्ष कर उसको नाप जहाँ...

बड़ा काफ़िला हुआ तो क्या, उठा पैर तू चल वहाँ....2

Utkarsh Sharma

जयपुर की पावन धरा पर जन्म लिया हैं मैंने, नाम उत्कर्ष शर्मा हैं मेरा।

लिखने का शौक तो बचपन से ही था, बस इंजीनियरिंग के बाद ये शौक, आदत में तब्दील हो गया।

मेरा तो यहीं कहना हैं कि -

सब नहीं कर सकते ये एहसास शायरी का जनाब।

ये तो वो नशा है जो कलम के जादूगर ही किया करते है।

कुछेक शब्दों का खेल नहीं है ये, ना ही नादान लोगो का पैंतरा चलता है यहां।

एक कला है ये, एक तस्वीर है जैसे कोई बेरंग सी, हम शायर जिसे अपना बना कर, रंग उसमें भरते है।

<u>एक स्त्री हैं वो।</u>

एक मां हैं वो, एक बहन हैं वो।
एक सखी हैं वो, जीवन संगिनी हैं वो।
एक स्त्री हैं वो।

रूप कई हैं उसके, कर्तव्य भी कई हैं।
सभी रूप निभाती बखूबी, कभी थकती नहीं हैं।
ना कभी शिकायत करती है वो, ना उसके मन का प्रेम कभी कम
होता हैं।
निश्छल हृदय की स्वामिनी हैं वो, उसका तो हर रूप दिव्य होता
है।

सह लेती हैं जुल्म इस जमाने के, गलत ना होते हुए भी।
हकदार जिस सम्मान की हैं वो, मिल ना पाया इस समाज से उसे
कभी।
पर कभी झुकना नहीं सीखा उसने, कंधे से कंधा मिलाकर चली हैं
वो।
ख़ूबसूरती और दृढ़ता का अनोखा संगम, गुलाब की एक हसीन
कली है वो।

अलौकिक हैं वो, विशाल हैं वो।
अपने आंचल में समेटे हुए, इस संसार की ढाल हैं वो।
एक स्त्री हैं वो।

Suman Gupta

Suman Gupta hailing from Oodlabari,West Bengal is a teacher/tutor by profession and a writer by passion. Writing is peace for her, a learner by nature, a true introvert, she has been the co author of three anthologies.

<u>बेटियां</u>

है ये बेटी किसी की,

आज बहू हो गई तो क्या हुआ।

कुसुम है वो एक आँगन की,

आज ज़मीन बदल गई तो क्या हुआ।

थोड़ा हक़ मा बाप का भी रहने देना उसपर,

अब कुछ नये रिश्ते जुड़ गए तो क्या हुआ।

करती थी वो जिद पापा से,

आज पति से करती है तो क्या हुआ।

हस्ती खिलखिलाती थी वो सहेलियों के साथ,

आज ननद के साथ जोरसे हस लिया तो क्या हुआ।

बेटी है वो उस घर की,

इस घर भी बन बेटी रह जाये तो क्या हुआ।

Alisha Kumari

S. Alisha Kumari is an English Professor. She has been working as English Language Trainer in various Institutes. She has published research articles in various publications and also co-author of various anthologies. Being a bibliophile, she loves to read and write a lot. You can follow her in instagram @alisha_kumari96 or mail her to k.alisha.666@gmail.com.

IRON-MAN
FE-MALE

Women Have strength in their weakness and weakness in the strength. They execute these things only before the person they trust and love most. For her everything is like give a try go for it or do it. She is one mystical creature made by God. He built her out of fire, during the Strom Filled with water and shaped the strict of air. She thinks like a scholar, works like a labour And rise like a Queen. They stand for others done to themselves. They control everyone, support and inspire to do things. Some women are like leaves that die during the winter but many of us don't know they come back during the season of spring. Being a beautiful flower they spread love and fragrance around them. They have this mystical view of seeing everything from the eyes of a mother. She appears and sees herself as a lass, girl, lady, women, mother, mother-in-law, sister, wife, grandmother, Godmother. She both shrinks and expands to fit into a certain situation but she is lively. Literate or illiterate women /mothers are a doctor. They are distinguished predictor and saviour of any situation. People say woman stands for purity, innocent and patient but no they stand also for brave, sincerity, loyal & as a multi-tasker. They say Women has two faces no they have a multi; it is based upon what attitude you use and which face you pick? When they are wrong or do wrong they try so hard to make it right. When the life pulls their leg for one inch, they climb a feet. And that's the power of women and incredible creature.

Leena AfshaIshrot

She's is Leena AfshaIshrot. She belongs to a small town from North East of India (Assam). A girl of twenty hardly talked with anyone. She reveals the truth of the society. She has participated in many anthologies.

<u>Life of a girl</u>

It is not easy to be a girl. She smiles in front of everyone, but no one can understand her deep pain. She has to tolerate many pains, starting from her menstrual pain till her pregnancy. Her first love is her father, who treats her as a princess. She has to play many roles in the society in order to survive. The patriarchal society gives many restrictions to her, but she has to be very bold and strong enough to overcome those obstacles. It is very difficult to trust people when her own relatives become hostile. Sometimes her family does not support her ideas and views, but she has to fight alone against them for her happiness and at that time everyone appreciates her worth. In the same place, we can see that on one hand, the women are worshiped as "Maa Saraswati", "Maa Durga", etc and on the other the brutal rape cases, murders, female feticides etc. In this patriarchal society nobody blames a man; I just want to question you all - why we girls are not raising any voice against these rapists? If we don't take any necessary step then it will be very difficult for the survival of our next generation in this planet. I don't blame only one gender that it is "his or her guilt" but, overall it is about a mentality, how a person thinks "everything begins in our mind". Okay fine, we assume that it is about dresses. Then why government does not ban those clothes? If it is a matter of our dresses, then why a small child is a victim? A small girl of five years old or so, she may don't even properly know how to wear a cloth! Damn! Even she has to struggle for a life! I would like to state that rapists cannot be called as humans. If he does not have the ability to bear pain, is it right to ruin other's life? After a girl is being raped, the rumour is spread all over the place that, she was this, she was that. But I would like to ask you a question; will a girl willingly gives a right to a stranger to touch her body, to open up her legs? The answer is obviously "No". Then why this blame only goes to a girl, who is unknown about this situation. Rather why it is not taught to boy, to respect a girl? A common thing is seen after a rape case is a candle march, in which rapists too join that by holding a candle in his hand. But it is a high time; we need to take a step to stop all those crimes. May be today we are ignoring as because they are strangers for us, but being a human they need our contribution to get rid out of it. So I wish everyone to help those rape victims as much as you can. As I am a girl I can feel the pain too.

Meenakshi

Meenakshi, she is from Punjab, India. She had done her masters in physics and currently, pursuing her B.Ed. She is an introvert. She loves to pens down her thoughts. She is fond of writing and love to spend some lone time with herself. According to her, find your own self is the most important part of our life and playing with words is the toughest work.

#Woman#

She knows when to keep quiet,
And when to fight.
She is kind unless,
You didn't mess with her mind.
She is an angel,
Until her demons are asleep.
She is one with multiple roles.
It's your destiny, what you hold
She is nothing compared to the man
She is beyond it
She is a WOMAN.

****

#She#

She is my mom,
She is also father to me.
She is a sister,
She is also brother to me.
She is a friend,
She is also my girlfriend to me.
She is the first woman of my life,
Who is everything to me.
****

#Everyday is yours

Oh woman!
You don't need to wait for a specific day
to celebrate your identity.
Be what you are.
Do what you want.
Get what is yours.
Show what you are,
And what you can be.
Every day is yours.

Gargi Bhattacharjee

Gargi Bhattacharjee, a writer, thinker, YouTuber.

She is a Post Graduate in Mathematics from Gauhati University, currently pursuing Post Graduation Diploma in Banking and Financial Services. She has written in more than 20 anthologies, which are basically as a co-author. And has edited and compiled an anthology book, "Voices of Change".

WOMEN: I want to be Celebrated Everyday

"We are women, we aren't weak", is the voice of all women, free from or captured by barriers. And by this we mean, when we wear the skin of women, we already hold a big responsibility. We, as women, want and hope to feel celebrated, happy and respected not just today but every day.

This is somewhat like a diary for me, being a women myself, would like to be very candid, unfiltered and unapologetic and this time without your permission. Therefore, before you read further let me put a disclaimer here, for I want and I will be discussing topics and situations, that are stereotyped, considered taboo, and all of these might make some of you cringe or frown. But please learn to accept and respect. Because it's the only way we can co-exist beautifully.

First thing first, actually everyday is a celebration in itself for any individual born or dead. It's just depends on the eyes and mind that see. And especially, we, as women take up lot of responsibilities physically, mentally, emotionally, socially and so on which can sometimes be a matter of struggle but the fact is we do not give up. We continue with the process.

A major credit goes to our conditioning and upbringing because, since childhood, we are taught to take up responsibilities, maintain home and families, and face all problems with a smile. We aren't allowed to complain, scream or shout and are asked to be sober and silent throughout the process.

Moreover, a female body goes through a lot. We are the bearer of pain and life at the same time. Our struggles with periods, cramps, PCOD, PCOS, pregnancy, labor pain, motherhood etc are all really difficult jobs which at times turn extreme. But, many a times, we are ignored, made to feel unimportant, after going through all the pain. So, at least we should learn to celebrate and empower ourselves.

Other than that, we are expected to match up to unnecessary and unnatural beauty standards, which if we follow or not, either way we are judged and criticized.

We have the constant pressure to look and project ourselves a certain way, but it should be stopped now. We are humans made of the same blood and flesh as you and it's natural to go through changes, gain or lose weight, have bad skin or hair days, be saggy and bloated. And we, women, should prefer not to change for others, but change only when we want to.

All we need is Love and Respect. Can we expect this from everyone in this world??? Not just on 8th March every year through whatsapp forwards but every day in real.

Set us free. Let us live. Teach our girls. Give them education and freedom. Let them join sports, science, army, art whatever they want.

 Lastly and most importantly, Say No to Rapes and Acid Attacks. Respect and Love Women. Be a Human First. Then you won't be able to attack anyone of any gender.

I won't say more. I rest my case here.

Aaysha Siddiqua

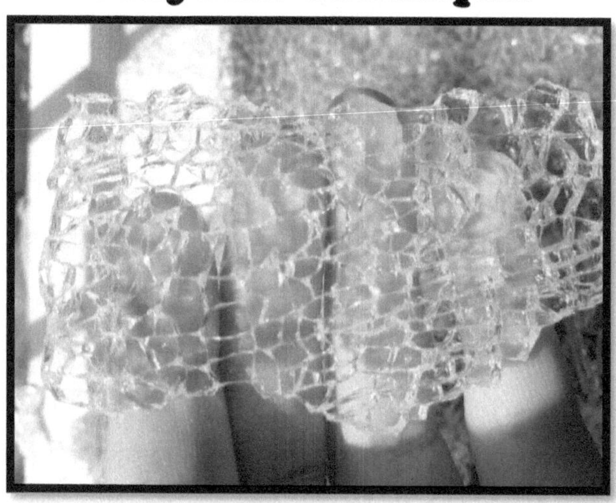

I am Aaysha Siddiqui, I'm from Surat. I'm graduated, I'm passionate to become a writer and love writing poems. I'm simple living girl with generous heart.

गम छुपाना बेवजह मुस्कुराना यह हुनर भी रखती है,

यह कभी अपने लिए नहीं अपनों के लिए ख्वाब देखती हैं ,

तुम माल व दौलत ना दो सिर्फ इज्जत का ताज पहना दो,

तुम्हारे साथ यह हर गम फिर खुशी से बसर करती है ,

नारी एक अच्छा ख्याल होती है पर उसे लोग बवाल समझते हैं,

वह लाजवाब होती है पर उसे मुश्किल सवाल समझते हैं,

खुद के वजूद को अधूरा छोड़ अपनों को मुकम्मल करती है,

सबर और बर्दाश्त से यह कमाल भी सिर्फ एक औरत करती है,

अपने दामन में नफरतों को समेट के मोहब्बत लुटाती है,

यह वह दिया है जो अंधेरों में खुद जल के रोनक ए फैलआती है।

Payal Lodha

Payal Lodha is young girl of 20, resident of Bhilwara, Rajasthan. She is pursuing her career as teacher and aspiring to bring a meaningful change in this world through her words

A letter to woman

Dear empowered woman,

Today I want to address you with your all attributes. I know it has not been an easy journey to come so far but believe in yourself. You have reached and you have broken all the so-called boundaries and parameters to make your identity. Being a girl I can understand it deeply that after walking a journey of miles, sometimes it still seems to us an uphill task to fight for self.

Nobody would have appreciated your all efforts ever and works to live for others but I know it is too hard to forget about self and devote self for others. It is not piece of cake which can be chewed easily but you have nailed it.

Dear women, you have done it. Yes, you have done it. If you can fight a war and win it for others then why can't you do it for self? You are an empowered woman, you can do it. You are the one who has sacrificed for her sleep and cried to sleep but did not let her child cry.

You are the one who worked for all 24 hours even after you shone like a star and the glitter of your face is more than the stars. After working for whole time, nobody could ever see the creases of exhausting day on your face then why can't you do it for self?

Yes this is true that God knows only a woman is patient, hardworking and powerful enough to bear any pain. So, God has given privilege to have a baby in her womb for 9 months not to a man.

If you could do it then believe yourself, you can walk on the way full of darkness, you can walk on the burnt coal to take the hardest exam of your life and to get succeeded.

You are more strengthened than man,

You are more patient and calm than man,

You are more intelligent than man,

You are actually more and more than a man!

So, don't ever feel or consider yourself dependent or weak. Just keep your head high, shoulders strong and most importantly keep being like a bold, beautiful, most shining soul who spreads happiness everywhere.

Thank you for everything you have done.

Payal Lodha

Chitransh Srivastava

My name is Chitransh Srivastava, I'm from Prayagraj. Currently I'm doing BA 3rd year from University of Allahabad. My hobbies are writing, reading, and cycling. I like whatever I feel and whatever I feel just write it.

कमजोर नहीं है वो तो ताकत कहलाती है

जब वह जन्म लेती है तब लड़की होने के कारण अपनी मां को खरी
खोटी सुनवाती है,
लेकिन कैसे कहूं उसे कमजोर मैं जो स्कूल जाने के ही उम्र मे गृहस्थी
चलाना सीख जाती है,
लड़के तो जाते हैं सिर्फ स्कूल लेकिन वो स्कूल और घर दोनों का काम
कर जाती है,
कमजोर नहीं है वो वो तो ताकत कहलाती है।

सहती है समाज का डर हर पल पर फिर भी वो मुस्कुराती है,
लोगो के कमेंट सुन कर भी आगे बढ़ जाती है,
कमजोर नहीं है वो वो तो ताकत कहलाती है।

फिर एक दिन ऐसा आता है अपने घर को छोड़ दूसरे के घर चले जाती
है,
अपने सपने को छोड़ अपनों का सपना पूरा करने लग जाती है,
कमजोर नहीं है वो वो तो ताकत कहलाती है।

अपना बचपना छोड़ कर एक बचपने को ले आती है,
उसे अपनी ममता दे कर एक माँ बन जाती है,
कमजोर नहीं है वो वो तो ताकत कहलाती है।

अपनी शिक्षा उसे दे कर एक काबिल इंसान बनाती है,
जीवन के हर राह को पार करना सिखाती है,
कमजोर नहीं है वो वो तो ताकत कहलाती है।

वैसे तो होता है दिल एकदम मासूम सा लेकिन जब बात ज्यादा बढ़
जाती है,
तो वो भी झांसी की रानी बन जाती है,
कमजोर नहीं है वो वो तो ताकत कहलाती है।

करती है सम्मान अपने पती का उसके लिए तो यमराज से भी लड़ जाती
है,
अपने पति की रक्षक बन कर सावित्री कहलाती है,
कमजोर नहीं है वो वो तो ताकत कहलाती है।

कैसे कह सकता हूँ कमजोर उन्हे जो मेरी माँ, मेरी बहन, मेरी बेटी
कहलाती है,
जो मुझे हर पल सही राह दिखाती है,
जो मुझे अपनी बात को कहना सिखाती है,
समाज भले ही कितना बुरा हो उनके साथ
लेकिन समाज में रहना सिखाती है,
कमजोर नहीं होती है वो वो तो हमारी ताकत कहलाती है।

नहीं है हम बिना उनके
वही तो हमारी ताकत कहलाती है,
हमारे दुखों को खुद सह कर एक महिला कहलाती है,
समझना नहीं उन्हे कमजोर कभी
क्यूँकि वही तो देवी दुर्गा कहलाती है,
कमजोर नहीं है वो वो तो ताकत कहलाती है।

Rekha Abbott

Date of birth- 10 -9 1975. New Delhi

Qualifications Graduation (Political science Hons) Delhi University

Early childhood education.

 Profession- Teacher, freelance author

Co author in the golden book of world record- "Pawan"

Co author in different anthologies with various Publications.

Email I'd - soniabbott75@g.mail.com

Social media page- abbottrekhawrites

I believe all this could have been possible because of my parents and family's constant support and motivation.

My motto- "दूसरों का अच्छा सोचो अपना अपने आप हो जाएगा"

मैं औरत हूं...

मैं औरत हूं

शक्ति मुझमें समाई है

काली , दूर्गा का मैं रूप हूं

मैं अबला नहीं सबला हूं

मैं जननी हूं

मेरी कोख में संसार समाया है

औरत और मर्द समान है

यह मेरी सोच का आधार है

बेटी ,बहन, मां , पत्नी

ना जाने कितने रूपों में ढली हूं

पर फिर भी आगे बढ़ी हूं

आज आत्मनिर्भर बन कर

खड़ी हूं

मैं समाज की हर कूरीति से लड़ी हूं

मैं औरत हूं और सम्पूर्ण हूं।

Himanshu Rawat

His name is Himanshu Rawat and he is a 19 years young singer, youtuber, writer, poet, lyricist from city beautiful Chandigarh.

<u>यह नए जमाने की नारी है</u>

यह नए जमाने की नारी है

यह सब पर भारी है

दस-दस लड़कों के बराबर

एक अकेली नारी है

यह नए जमाने की नारी है

यह सब पर भारी है

मदर टेरेसा, साइना नेहवाल, हिमा दास

कल्पना चावला, रानी लक्ष्मीबाई और ऐश्वर्या राय जैसे उदाहरणों

से भरी ये दुनिया हमारी है

यह नए जमाने की नारी है

यह सब पर भारी है

हर क्षेत्र में हर व्यवसाय में हर काम में अपनी बुलंदी का झंडा

वह लहरारी है

यह नए जमाने की नारी है

यह सब पर भारी है

विश्व स्तर पर वह भारत को आगे बढ़ा रही है

यह नए जमाने की नारी है

यह सब पर भारी है

लड़का और लड़की के भेदभाव को
वह खत्म करती जा रही है
यह नए जमाने की नारी है
यह सब पर भारी है

ना कभी वह हारी थी
न हारेगी
ना हारी है
यह नए जमाने की नारी है
यह सब पर भारी है
दस-दस लड़कों के बराबर
एक अकेली नारी है
यह नए जमाने की नारी है
यह सब पर भारी है

Rishav Banerjee

This is Rishav Banerjee, hailing from Kolkata, West Bengal. He is a student of class 12 with a keen interest in cooking, drawing and dancing. He keeps a knack on reading books and has a strong grip on writing. He actively works as an activist of LGBTQ community to fight for their rights. He recently has achieved the prestigious position of CHIEF CITY AUTHOR from Kolkata by TGIWC Community. Moreover, he wants to become a good chef in near future and change the world with his persona.

<u>WOMEN THE ULTIMATE STRENGTH</u>

 Women's Day is all about commemorating these extraordinary women and showing them how much we love, respect and what the actual significance of them in our society is!! The existence of women has many stages like growing as a daughter and steeping towards teenage!! As a mother, she invariably cares for us with utmost love and care!! Being a sister she is your promising companion. As a wife, she has many responsibilities to confirm, still, she is strong and loving.
She is Wonderful in each role that she plays in our lives and helps us to reach our individual goals!!! She makes us glad and smiles even if she is in grief. Life is nothing without them
Happy Women's Day to all the women who is in this planet
Devoted in love with someone from Canada CA (far away from 14,000 Km)

Ishant Nikure

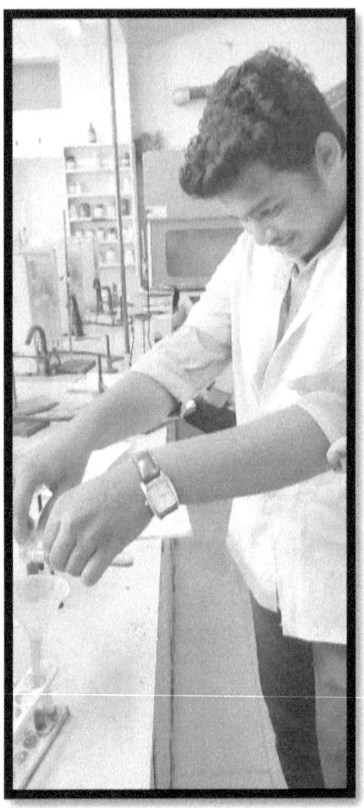

Ishant Nikure here. He is a student of life science and lives in Nagpur, Maharashtra. He also teaches biology to 10th STD, he has experience of writing since last 10 years. He is an artist, poet and writer. He has published his 1st book in Marathi language. He loves to write in English, Hindi and Marathi language.

वो स्त्री होती हैं

वो अपने माँ बाप छोडकर,

पराये घर में आती हैं|

वो अंजान लोग को अपना बनाती हैं|

वो अपने सारे दुःखो को भुलाकर परिवार की खुशिया धुंढती हैं,

वो माँ, बेहेन, पत्नी, बेटी और देश का गौरव कहलाती हैं|

जो खुद की परवाह ना करते हुये,

अपने परिवार को बनाती है|

वो बहु घर की लक्ष्मी होती,

वो ऑफिसर, अभिनेत्री, राष्ट्रपती और आदिशक्ती होती है,

वो कोई और नहीं, एक संपूर्ण सक्षम स्त्री होती है|

Vaishnavi Devi

I am Vaishnavi Devi... Pursuing my under graduation in English literature... Co Author of anthologies...The path you choose, overwhelmed souls and Reminiscing the year... Writing is my passion... Love to pen my feelings and Emotions on paper...To colour my life with colourful ink... Love's to Imagine... Dreamer!

<u>STRONG WOMEN</u>

Young women...Born with curse,
But born with courage...
You are born beautiful
To give the world your smile's
Of happiness...
She smiles in her troubles too
As she troubles in her education
Her wishes buried in the homes
As the ashes...
Treated as slaves for men...
But she remains silent...
And gave sparkling smile...
She troubles her body and soul
To give birth for a child
As the flower blossoms...
She Smiles and accepts these pains...
But scolded for giving birth for a girl child...
She gives her soul and heart
But what she gets in return?
Nothing but treated as garbage and slaves...
Bears all her troubles and lives in this hard world...
No matter how bad her life is...
She lives for her family...as to take care of them
Is she weak? She resembles the face of sacrifice and strong...

Priyanka Bose

Priyanka Bose From Odisha loves to write short poems and articles. According to her, beauty attracts the eye but piece of writing captures the heart... Though she is from commerce background but love and passionate to enlighten the society through her writings.

No woman's day, first celebrate man's day. No appeasing me, first learn to behave.... Why treating me specially? Why not equally? Am I a species? Fading gradually! Worshipping goddess, killing daughter! Get lost hypocrisy, please don't bother........

Deepak Anantha Rao

आप का जन्म केरल राज्य के कोट्टयम जिल्ला के पूञ्जर नामक गाव में।आप हिंदी एवं मलयालम भाषा के एक कवि,गायक एवं ग़ज़ल शायर।एमए.,एमफिल.,बीएड्.,अनुवाद में स्नातकोत्तर डिप्लोमा एवं बी एड्. यताएँ। हिंदी के राज्य स्तरीय अनुसंधान आदि शैक्षिक योग्(गणित) प्रशिक्षक और एक कुशल वक्ता।स्कूल कलोत्सव के राज्य स्तरीय विधि साझा) चमन चमन के फूल :कर्ताओं में एक है। प्रकाशित कृतियाँ हंस प्रकाशन (काव्य संकलन, नई दिल्ली,यू आर एक्सपेक्शनल (अंग्रेजी एवं हिंदी साझा काव्य संकलन),'डाण्ट वाक अलोन, वेन यू हाव फण्ड्स बिसाइड' बुक स्कुविरल, फणिटिक्स पब्लिकेशन्स नई दिल्ली। अभी केरल राज्य के, एक सरकारी हाईस्कूल के अध्यापक।

<u>दादी माँ, प्यार का दूसरा नाम</u>

कौतूहल के दो नयन उनके पैरों तले छिप के

ममता एवं प्यार से अपनी काल्पनिक दुनिया ढूँढते।

तब दादी कहती थी हर बच्चा ईश्वर होता है।

सुनकर बहुत खुश हो गया तब कि

मैं भी ईश्वर हूँ, सभी से प्यार आज़मायिशता हूँ।

इसलिए दादी मुझे बहुत पसंद थी मेरी जान थी।

उनका रूप मुझे अच्छा लगा था और रंग भी

सुनहरे बालों की लटों में छुपना कभी मेरा आदत भी।

झुके नयनों में रोशनी थोड़ी भी कम नहीं थी।

रात को आसमान मे चमकते सितारों जैसे

उनकी आखें भी सदा चमकती थी।

वो देखकर बैठना मुझे बहुत पसंद था।

दादी मेरे लिए अपनी अनोखी दुनिया थी।

प्यार का पुल और हमारा झक झक चुक चुक।

आपस में प्यार जताते कभी कभी झगडा करते

हम दो बच्चे, मैं और अपनी प्यारी दादी

असल में तो घर का दिया दादी ही होती है।

हमेशा मुस्कुराते सभी को एक सूत्र बाँघते।

बीते हुए कल को अनुभव की कसौटी

पर कसके लगातार मेरी दादी चलती रहती।

परिवार तो सदा सही धारा में और मैं सदा खुश भी।

न कोई ऐसा पल नहीं रहा मेरे बचपन में,

ना ऐसा कोई रात भी न रहा,

बिना कोई कहानी और मनमानी के।

हमेशा मेरी दादी चलती फिरती एक किताब थी।

जिसका पन्ना जितना भी पलटे समास न हो जायें।

अपनी प्यारी दादी और अपना मधुर बचपन

हमेशा बारात लेकर आती है अब भी

मेरे सुनहरे यादों में,

बचपन एक खोया हुआ सत्य ॥

Rohan Tyagi

Rohan Tyagi...
A guy who accepts success and failures from open arms...
Music is what refreshes him and cricket is what he loves...
Writing is what comes with every breath of his...
I am from Delhi doing B tech from IP University....
21 years of age and just living the life as it is a kingdom of his own...
Pen name- RT♡
Insta handle - @zindagii_ka_safar

Happy Women's Era

तुम हीर नहीं नायाब हीरा हो इस जहान का...

तुम कोई चीज नहीं नुमाइश की...

सहारा हो अपने हर रिश्ते का...

तुम कोई आजमाईश नहीं...

तोहफा हो उस खुदा का...

तुम एक ख़ास दिन की मोहताज नहीं...

इबादत हो हर दिन का...

तुम कोई आम हस्ती नहीं...

एक पैग़ाम हो इंसानियत का।।

Roshni Panjabi

Hello, Roshni Panjabi here. While I enjoy a good amount of writing daily, I am currently pursuing BMS in finance, last year. I reside in Mumbai, Maharashtra. I own my writing page @hearttosoul_

<u>Opinions</u>

Things which I don't say out loud to society that I don't care about your opinions anymore, because I am here today with the help of my parents and my confidence not by your opinions.

****

<u>Women's Day</u>

By posting women's day status or wishing them doesn't make any person a gentleman, the true women's day celebration is to respect and take care of the feelings of the women in your life.

Aryan Verma

This is Aryan Verma, an introvert, born & raised in Muzaffarpur, Bihar, pursuing Bachelor's degree in the field of Arts. From past four years, he has been indulged in writing though he never thought to share & kept this as a hobby. But now when life showed all colors, he finally came out few months back with his writings to the world. Writing for him is to express his feeling through words. Being a passionate writer, it's a dream to turn his passion into a thriving career as a professional writer. He has progressed quite a bit to formulate longer and more complex stories and sharing them with much larger audiences.

You can read his blogs at:

www.aryanverma.com

एक स्त्री ऐसे ही नहीं सर्वगुण संपन्न कहलाती हैं।

चुप हो जाती है वो,
समाज की बंदिशों को देख कर।
फिर भी हर जगह अपना परचम लहराती हैं।
एक स्त्री ऐसे ही नहीं सर्वगुण संपन्न कहलाती हैं।

भाग-दौर भरी ज़िन्दगी,
दिन भर की थकान।
घर ही उसकी ज़मीन,
घर ही उसका आसमान।

वो कहते हैं न,
अगर घर का स्तम्भ है पुरुष,
तो स्त्री बुनियाद हैं।
और इन दोनों के मेल मात्र से ही घर आबाद हैं।

कमज़ोर न समझना उसे,
वही दुर्गा का रूप हैं, वही काली का स्वरुप हैं।
चुप रह कर सब सहन जरूर करती है,
पर हर हालात से भिड़ने की ताकत भी रखती हैं।

कहते है वो खुदा की सबसे प्यारी रचना हैं,
सुन्दर हैं वो रूप में, कृत्य से अन्नपूर्णा हैं।
वो जो हो घर में तो लक्ष्मी,
और विद्वानों में सरस्वती होती हैं।

वो जननी हैं हर कुल की,उसी से ये संसार हैं।
उसकी महिमा का तो खुद खुदा भी शुक्रगुज़ार हैं।

वो शक्ति हैं, वो ही अमर्त्य का वरदान हैं।
वो ही तो होती हर घर की शान हैं।
खुद से पहले हमेशा दुसरो का सोचती हैं,
एक स्त्री ऐसे ही नही सर्वगुण संपन्न कहलाती हैं।

Sukrutha B

An unconditional extrovert and an updating retrograde. A learner forever. An emotional extremist.

<u>Women:</u>

With all that you have you can only give;
With all that you gain you can only give.

You are a miracle;
You are a magic;
You are a motivation;
You are a marvel

Never can I ever overpower you;
Never can I ever overestimate you;
Never can I ever over speculate you;
Never can I ever overpressure you;

With all that you have given I have gained;
With all that you have given I have grown;
With all that you have given I have got better;
With all that you have given I have got a great life.

Abhishek V Jaiswal

A 21 year old passionate writer from Amravati, Maharashtra. Doing his graduation in civil engineering & also the founder of budding writer's community named Lekhaks world.

वो कहते है ना हर कामियाब आदमी के कामयाबी के
पीछे एक औरत होती है।

और ये बात भी उतनी ही सही है क्यों की हम उनकी मौजूदगी के
बिना कोई मुकाम हासिल करने के बारे में सोच भी नहीं सकते।

अगर कभी माँ हमें ज़िंदगी के रास्तों पर चलना ना सिखाती तो
ज़िंदगी के रास्ते ना जाने कितने मुश्किल हो जाते।

माना कि बहने राखी बांध कर रक्षा वचन लेती हो पर आज वे खुद
देश की सरहदों पर देश की रक्षा कर रही है।

और पत्नी सिर्फ गृहणी तक
सीमित न रहकर अनेक क्षेत्रों में
अपना नाम कमा रही है।

इतने सारे रिश्ते और जिम्मेदारीयो में बंधे रहने के बावजूद वो अपने
कर्तव्यो को बखूबी निभा रही है। और यही इस युग की नारी है।

www.ingramcontent.com/pod-product-compliance
Lightning Source LLC
LaVergne TN
LVHW091232180726
843490LV00006B/2056